W9-AXF-262

BRIGHTLY
WOVEN

BRIGHTLY WOVEN

THE GRAPHIC NOVEL

ALEXANDRA BRACKEN

ADAPTED BY
LEIGH DRAGOON

ART BY
KIT SEATON

LETTERING BY
CHRIS DICKEY

Quercus

QUERCUS CHILDREN'S BOOKS

First published in Great Britain in 2021 by Hodder & Stoughton
First published in the US in 2020 by Hyperion, an imprint of Disney Book Group

1 3 5 7 9 10 8 6 4 2

Adapted from the novel *Brightly Woven*

A CIP catalogue record for this book
is available from the British Library.

ISBN 978 1 786 54156 7

Designed by Marci Senders

Printed and bound in China

The paper and board used in this book
are made from wood from responsible sources.

Quercus Children's Books
An imprint of
Hachette Children's Group
Part of Hodder & Stoughton
Carmelite House
50 Victoria Embankment
London, EC4Y 0DZ

An Hachette UK Company
www.hachette.co.uk

www.hachettechildrens.co.uk

For my parents, for everything.
And for Carlin, the reason this story wove itself together in my mind.
—A.B.

To all the authors who've generously allowed me to be a guest in their worlds, both as a writer and as a reader.
—L.D.

For George, my dear friend and mentor,
who taught me to practice patience and seek peace.
—K.S.

Kingdom of Palmarta
Village of Cliffton

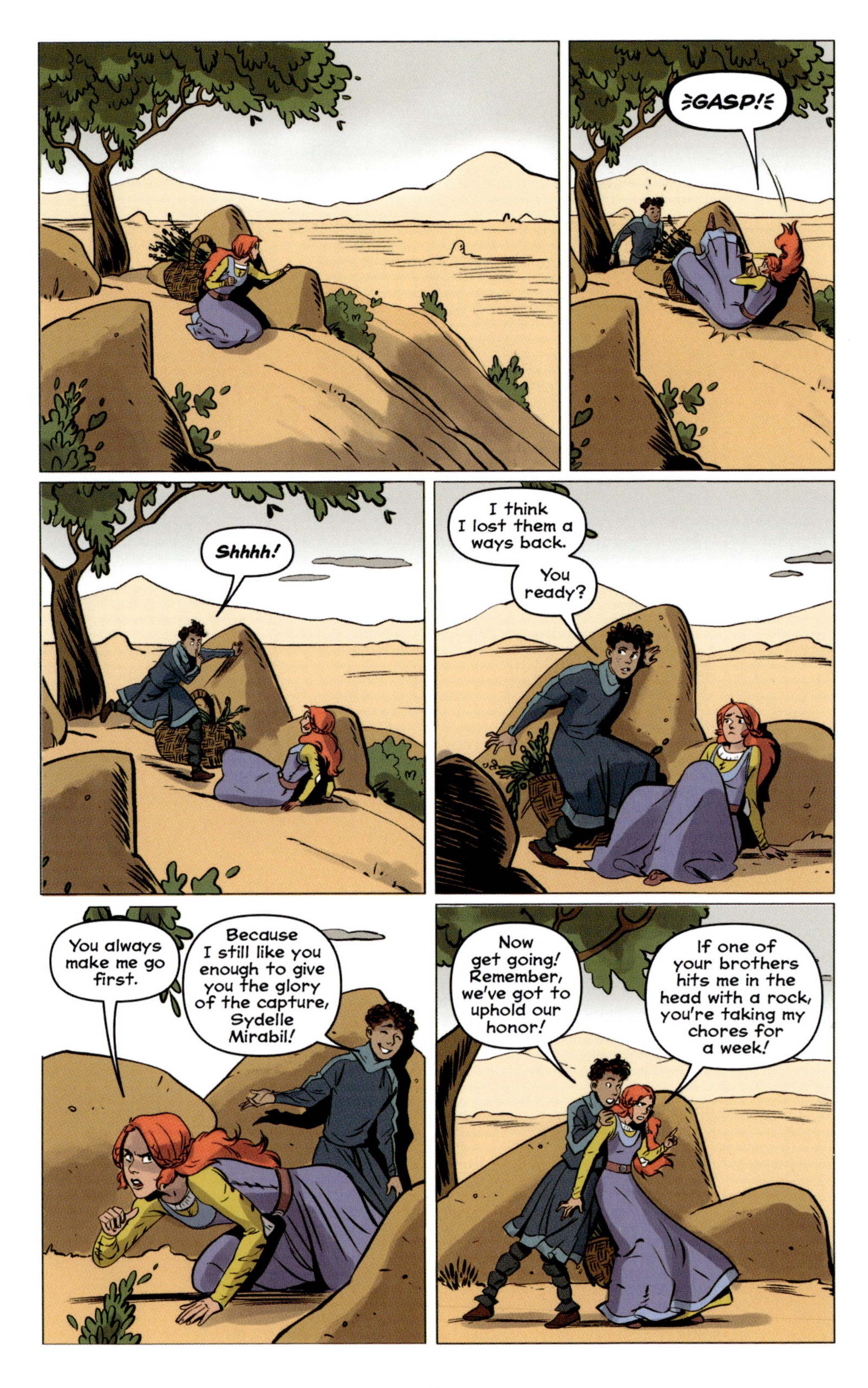
GASP!
Shhhh!
I think I lost them a ways back.
You ready?
You always make me go first.
Because I still like you enough to give you the glory of the capture, Sydelle Mirabil!
Now get going! Remember, we've got to uphold our honor!
If one of your brothers hits me in the head with a rock, you're taking my chores for a week!

OW!!!

You little demons!

RUUURUUUUMMMMBBBBLLLEE!
Wha–?

I can't believe it!
I know! It hasn't rained in ten years!
Hurry, take the twins back to the village!
What about you?
I've got to get my basket!
?!

Mmmn!!!
Please don't scream. I'm going to let you go, but don't scream, all right?
WHOCK!
Please, wait!

What are you doing up here? Are you from the village? From Cliffton?
Why? Are you a tourist or something?
I assure you, I'm a great appreciator of dry wit, but we've got to get out of here.

Wha--

SYDELLE!

It's all right! I'm Wayland North. I'm working with the Sorceress Imperial and Wizard Guard.

The Sorceress Imperial?!

Sydelle, go wait in your room.
But--
Please, go!

Are you the one responsible for this rain?

Yes. There are Austeran soldiers after me. I'm hoping the rain will muck up the roads enough to slow them down.
Well, regardless, we're grateful.
Every wizard the capital ever sent us failed to fix our drought.

It's of vital importance I get my report to the capital as quickly as possible.
I have proof the country of Auster is not responsible for our king's assassination.
In *one* month's time, Queen Eglantine's calling a council that'll vote on whether or not we go to war with Auster.
My report's the only thing that's got even half a chance to stop it.
But why don't you send your report through the mail service?! Wouldn't it be faster?
Yes! Surely something this-- this *important*...
There are people trying to stop me, and my magic is the only reason I've been able to stay ahead of them.
In Astraea's name, we'll give you anything you need-- food, supplies, a good mule...

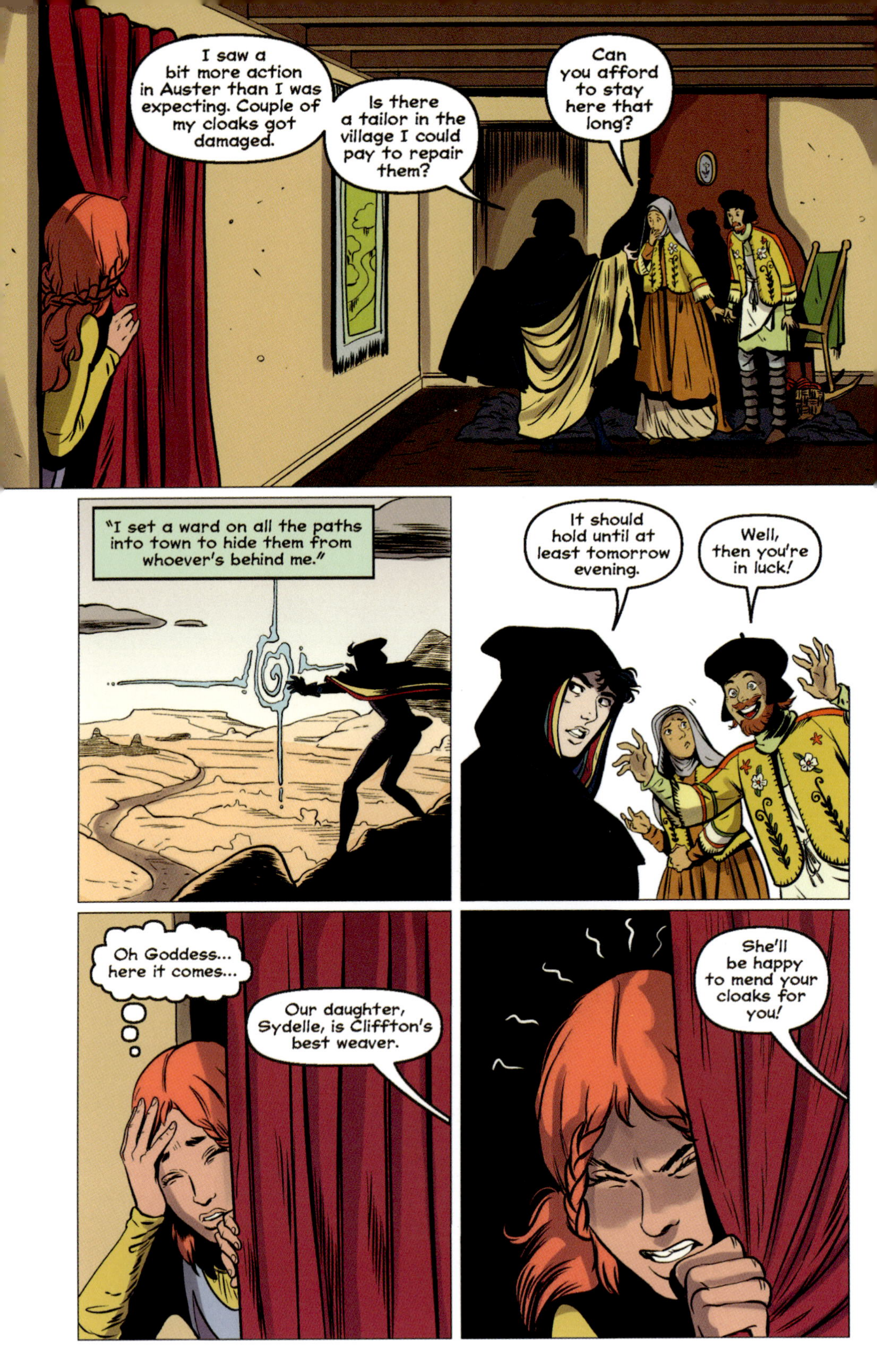
I saw a bit more action in Auster than I was expecting. Couple of my cloaks got damaged.
Is there a tailor in the village I could pay to repair them?
Can you afford to stay here that long?
"I set a ward on all the paths into town to hide them from whoever's behind me."
It should hold until at least tomorrow evening.
Well, then you're in luck!
Oh Goddess... here it comes...
Our daughter, Sydelle, is Cliffton's best weaver.
She'll be happy to mend your cloaks for you!

Sydelle!
You don't mind, do you?
No, Father, of course not.
Go ahead and show him to your room. You can sleep in ours tonight.
You don't really have to mend them.
It's no trouble, North.
Do you know anything about magic?
Only what's in my schoolbooks.

Well, I need these cloaks to use my magic, and they won't work if they're not repaired carefully.
Magic or not, I know what I'm doing. I'll be careful.
How about one to start?
Do you really need *all* those cloaks? Why not just one?
Each color matches a type of magic. The colors have to be in equal amounts to work properly.

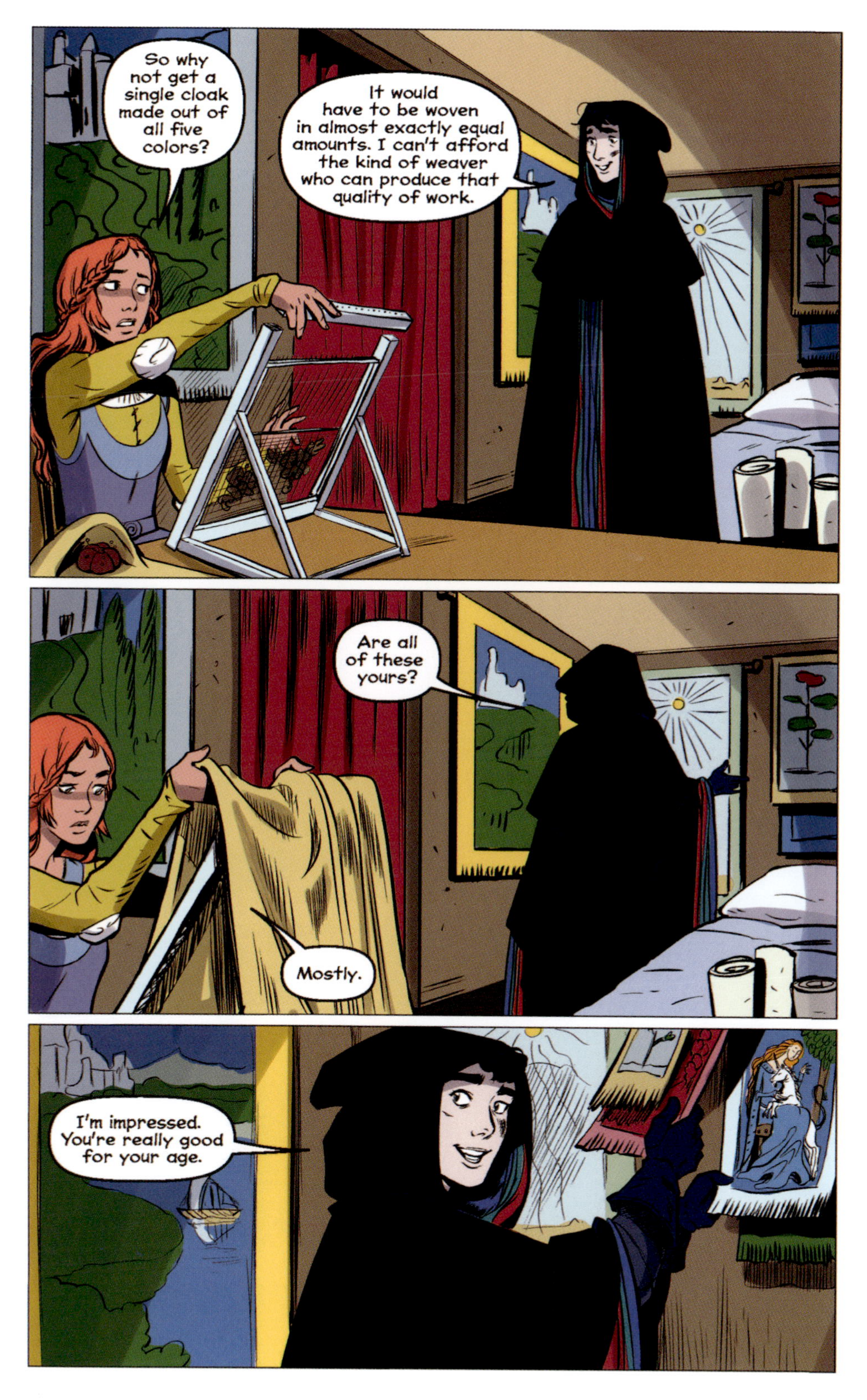
So why not get a single cloak made out of all five colors?
It would have to be woven in almost exactly equal amounts. I can't afford the kind of weaver who can produce that quality of work.
Are all of these yours?
Mostly.
I'm impressed. You're really good for your age.

I'll have you know, I just turned fourteen.
What about you? Aren't you a little young to be a wizard?
I'll have *you* know, *I* just turned fifteen.
And I have good taste in art.
Like this one! Wow! This is a really good likeness of the capital! Have you ever been to Provincia?
Of course not.
What? Why not?
You're certainly a good enough weaver to find work and support yourself in the city.
Because I can't.

You know, we're not all wizards. We can't just go flitting in and out of places on a whim.
We have families that need us, responsibilities--
That's not really fair.
Wizards have a lot of responsibility, too. We're basically born into service to the realm.
Your magic is a gift from the goddess Astraea. You should be grateful to be able to use it in service of the people, as she intended.
Well, if the Austerans win a war against Palmarta, my future's not going to look so rosy.
Their first order of business will be to wipe all us wizards out. It's what their goddess, Salvala, demands.
I know about Salvala. Just because Cliffton's a small village doesn't mean I didn't get a good education.

There. I'm done.
That's nice work.
But now comes the real test.

THUMP!

Whoa! Are you okay?
O-of course. I'm fine.
Excellent work, Madam Weaver.
It's no problem. Have a good night, North.
Whew
WHUMF!

BA-DUM
BA-DUM

Sydelle? Are you all right?
Just a strange dream.

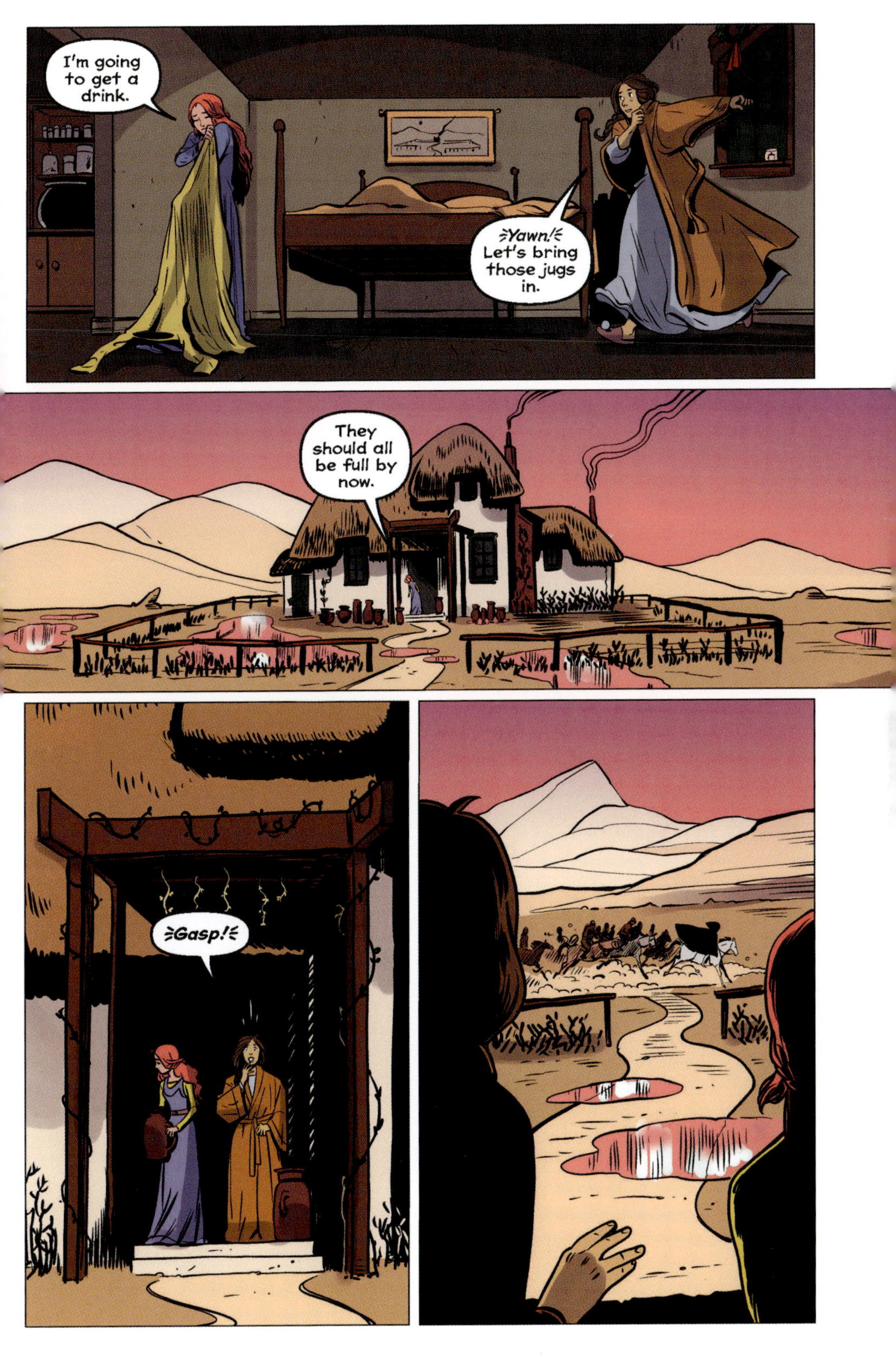
I'm going to get a drink.
Yawn! Let's bring those jugs in.
They should all be full by now.
Gasp!

Wake up Wayland! Tell him the Austerans are here!
Wait, where are you going?
To ring the temple bell and warn everyone!
North! North, get up! The soldiers are coming!
Wha? Already?!

You know the hills around here pretty well?
Of course! I live here, don't I?
Good.
Hey! What are you doing with that?!
KLONG KLONG KLONG
The bell--
We need to go *now.*

Hey--

Where's the main road?
Hey, stop!
How can you just leave them there?! You should help them!
There's nothing I can do!
You're a **wizard**!

The best way we can help Cliffton is by getting me out of here.
This is your fault! They only attacked us because of you!
I know. But the farther away I am, the higher the odds those soldiers will move on and leave Cliffton alone.
What do you need me for?! Just swirl your cloak and magic yourself away!
Firstly, I'm exhausted, and twisting is a dangerous spell without much room for error.
And every time I use magic, it makes it easier for others to track me.
You can't force me to go with you.
Sigh
Look, Syd...
Earlier you were complaining about your responsibilities. Well, now you've got a choice.
You can help me get to the capital and deliver a message that will prevent an actual war--
--or you can go back down there and wait things out with your family.

Fine.
I'll make sure you get to the main road.
Good! Now that that's settled--
Er...is there a way to... fold this up? It's a bit awkward.
All right. Let's get going.

And don't think I don't know you only brought my loom because you're hoping to get free work out of me.
Aha...
It's that obvious?

So, what now? Which way?
What do you mean, which way? Look at the sun!
That's back the way we came--
And that's *east!* You know, toward the capital?!

I don't have a great sense of direction.
I'm...going to have to lead you the whole way, aren't I?
How about just to the next major city? Dellark is only a few days' travel from here.
Only because we're going to prevent a war! But we need to work something out right now.
I'm not cooking, I'm not cleaning, and I'm not fire-starting or latrine-digging. I'm here to do one thing: make sure you get to the capital before the vote.
And you're going to pay me three florins in return for each cloak I repair.
I knew I could count on you, Syd.
Sydelle. My name's ***Sydelle.***

TWO DAYS LATER...
DELLARK...

I have a little money if you want to sleep inside tonight.
There's a really nice place about half a mile farther up--
THE SWEATY GOOSE
Here.
Ooookay...
Here it is!

I'll get you a room.
FLUMP!
Dinner! It's on the house!
CLATTER!
I worked out a deal with the innkeeper. I used a tiny bit of magic to kill all their roaches and bedbugs.
Go on, dig in!

Can I have the room key? I just want to wash up first.
Gulp!

BUMP!
Hey!
Has anyone ever told you your hair is the same color as the goddess Salvala's?
What about it?
Oh, nothing. Just remarking on it, that's all.

I know that boy you're with.
Yeah?
I know he calls himself a wizard. He's a fraud.
I can show you some *real* magic.
What?!
Kof!!

Gasp!
Father!
Why can't they hear me?!

NO!
Astraea, help me...
SYDELLE!
Wh- what--
Earthquake! We've gotta get out of here!

It's stopped.
Thank Astraea.

You ready to get out of here?
Definitely.
North, what was that?! That wizard--he sent me back to Cliffton! I saw my house burning!
That was Dorwan.
The mastermind behind the king's assassination.

I tried to blast him with a fireball, but he got away.
What?!
Here, drink this. It'll help, believe me.

Dorwan knows I have information that could stop the war. He's been tracking me since Auster, trying to stop me.
That trick he pulled on you was pure dark magic. It's forbidden by the Wizard Guard.

Hey, what's that thing?

Ahhh!

WHACK!

POOOF!
A magic-eater! Dorwan must have sent it after me right before I blasted him.
Look! You can see where it drained the magic.
Here, let me see.
I can fix this.
Ugh! They're worse than ticks!

You'll have to work on it tonight.
Right now, we need to get going. We should put as much distance between us and Dorwan as possible.
Lead us, young hero!
You know, we're practically the same age.
Ahem! I mean, ***"Deign to lead us, oh wise one!"***
You still haven't said where.
Oh! Ah, yes, of course.
Examine your maps and select the shortest path to the fine city of ***Fairwell!!!***

FAIRWELL
It's so bright!
Wow.
fromager
cordouanier
VICTUALS

I knew Fairwell was famous for its glass, but I didn't realize there'd be so much!
I can't wait to see your face when we get to Provincia.
Prepping for war?
I'm not going to let it come to that.

BOOKS
Come on. This is the place.
A bookshop? What do we need in here?
Not a "what"...
...a "who."

Wayland! My friend!
Where have you been all this time?!
I was about ready to organize a search party!
WHEEZE!
Government business.
Owain, this is my lovely new assistant, Syd.
--elle.
Well met, dear lady. Owain Gallant, journeyman knight, at your service.
That's not really his last name.
Perhaps not! But it is a worthy goal!
How are things around here?
You know how it is.

Did some odd jobs for my grandmother, new shingles, a little painting, wrote reviews for a few upcoming books. Things like that.
OOKS
Owain keeps a few of my things when I go out of town.
North, there's a letter here for you from Lady Aphra.
Who is Lady Aphra?
A family friend. She lives up in the mountains, in Arcadia. She fosters kids there.

Whoa.
NORTH
WAYLAND NORTH
"A few things"?
He keeps promising to take most of it out of here.
Sod it all!
What is it?
"We've been attacked by what appears to be a demon made of light that has taken the form of a wolf. The children are terrified. We fear it will strike again soon."

I *knew* Dorwan would bait me, but I *never* thought he'd send a demon out after kids.
He's such a coward!
We have three days until the vote. If we leave first thing tomorrow morning, that'll give me all the time I need to take care of Dorwan.
Owain, go on ahead of us to Provincia. You'll be my backup plan in case Sydelle and I are delayed. Tell the Sorceress Imperial to do everything she can to delay the vote until I get there!
North, I'm just a freelancer! They'll never listen to me!
I'll write you a letter of introduction.

I'm going to write to my parents.
I need to let them know I'm all right.
I don't blame you. If it were my family, I'd probably send a letter.
Well... maybe not *my* family.
You don't get along with them?
Let's just say that's a thread better left unpulled.

Dear Mother and Father, I'm all right. I wish I could say more. I don't know when I'll be able to write again.
I love you both, and I hope this letter reaches you and finds you well.
Love, Sydelle
Colar Monticelli
Vol. 2
A Treatise on Advanced Theurgy

What's that you got there? Monticelli? Ugh! Dry, boring, **and** hopelessly out of date.
Here. Read this one instead. It's well written and much more informative.
Plus, that's my personal copy.
Proper Instructions for Young Wizards
Fifth Edition

That dream again!

It probably doesn't mean anything.

THE NEXT MORNING
I'm going to twist us there.
Wait, isn't that too far?!
I can do it. It'll wipe me out, but I can do it.
North, what if that's what Dorwan wants?! To get you to exhaust yourself?
It's worth the risk.

North?
Wayland!
Help! We need some help!

Cheer up, girl. I've known Wayland for a long time. He's come through worse.
Uuurrrrggggghhhhhhhh

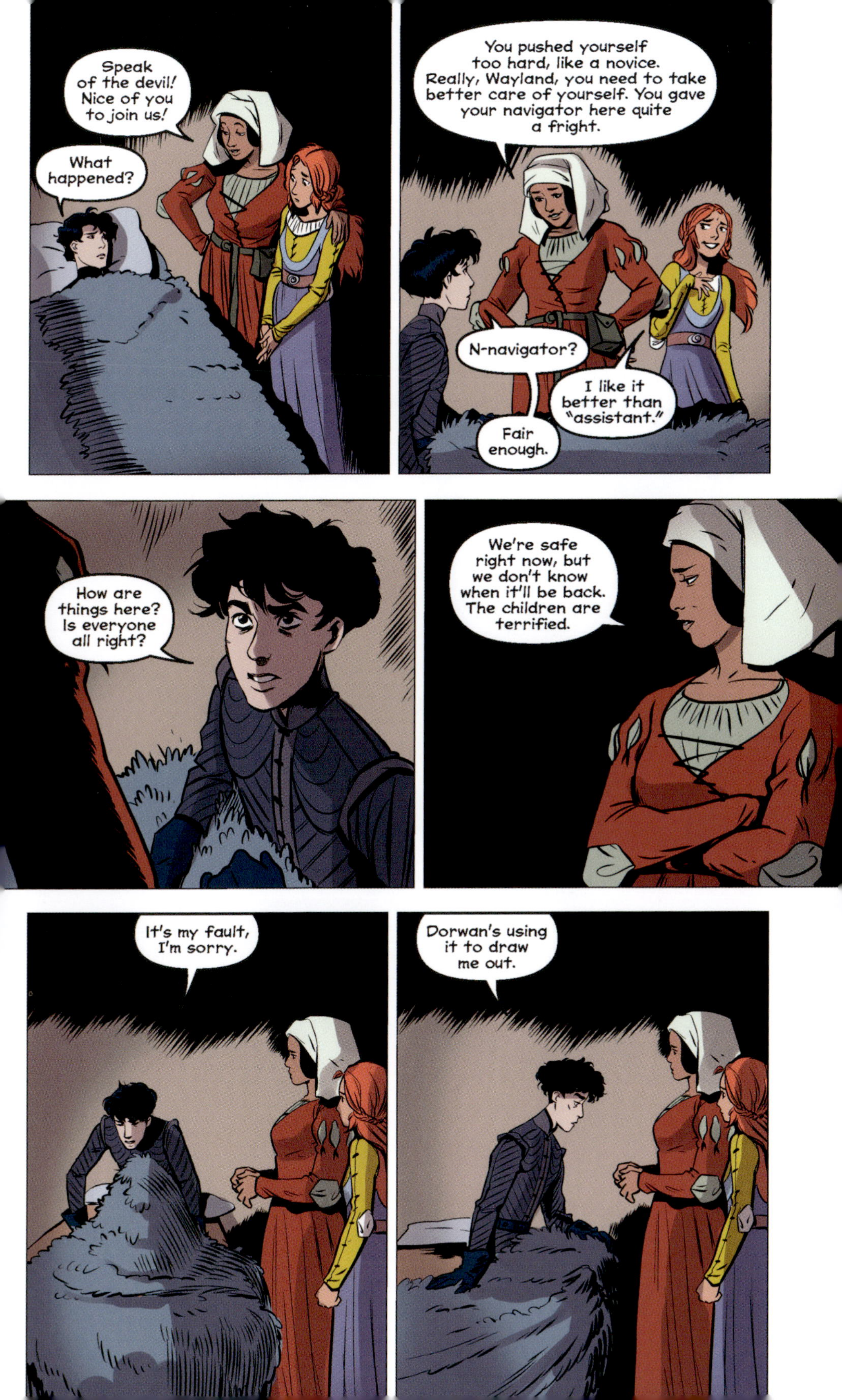
Speak of the devil! Nice of you to join us!
What happened?
You pushed yourself too hard, like a novice. Really, Wayland, you need to take better care of yourself. You gave your navigator here quite a fright.
N-navigator?
I like it better than "assistant."
Fair enough.
How are things here? Is everyone all right?
We're safe right now, but we don't know when it'll be back. The children are terrified.
It's my fault, I'm sorry.
Dorwan's using it to draw me out.

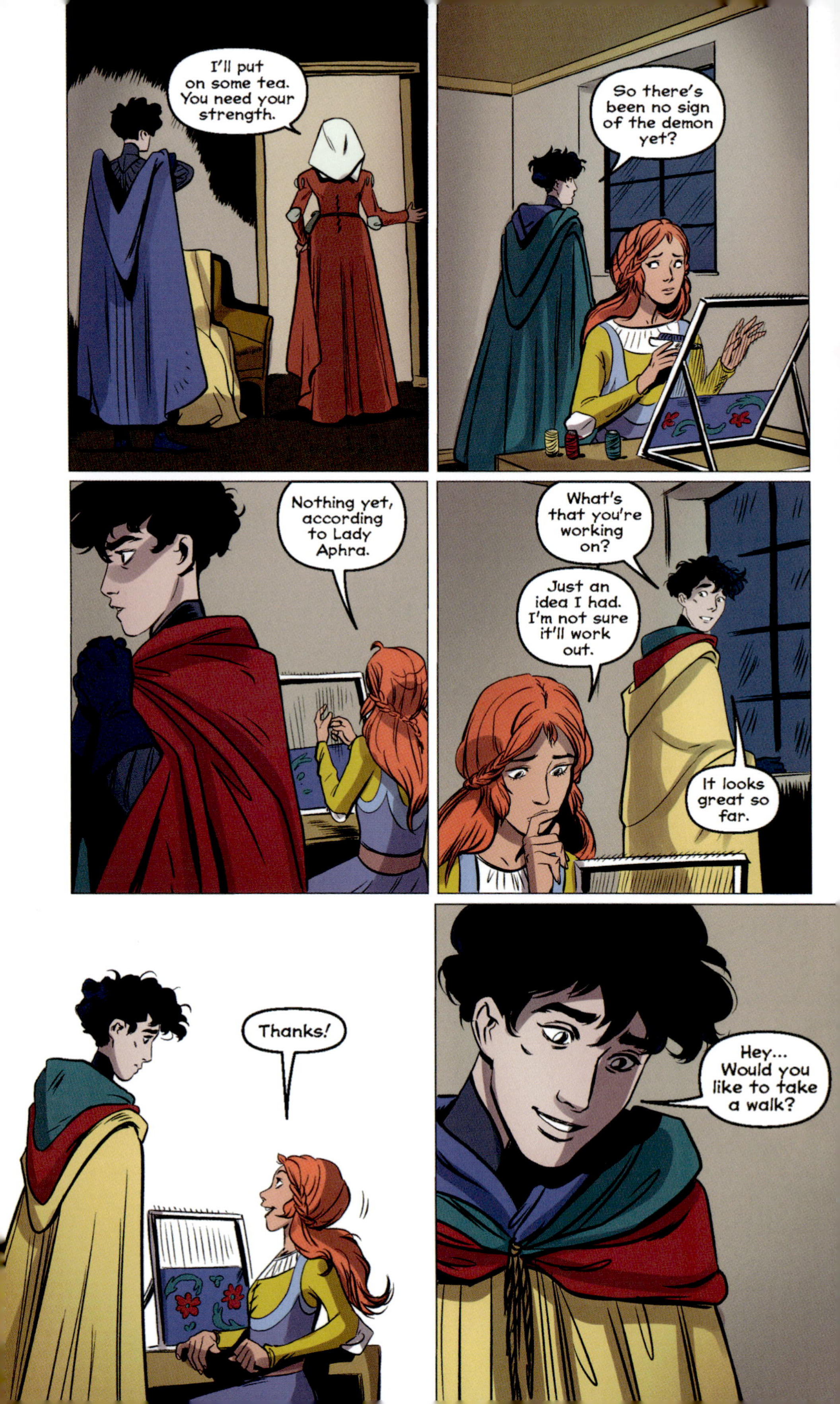
I'll put on some tea. You need your strength.
So there's been no sign of the demon yet?
Nothing yet, according to Lady Aphra.
What's that you're working on?
Just an idea I had. I'm not sure it'll work out.
It looks great so far.
Thanks!
Hey... Would you like to take a walk?

Brrr! By Astraea! It's so cold!
I forgot that you grew up in the desert.
Better?
Much! But don't you need it?

Nah. Besides, it suits you.
What, red and red?

It matches your hair.

Mmmm! Smells like snow.
Really?! Is this what it smells like?
You've never seen snow before?
Well... no.
Right! Desert!
Hey, it *is* snowing! You're like a walking good-luck charm!
It's so... small!
Ha! Yeah, well, when you have millions of them falling for hours, they pile up quick.

North? Is this... normal?
It's Dorwan! Get back to the house and lock the door!
What?!
Wait!
Your cloak!

CRASH!
NORTH!

SNARL!

NORTH!
Ah, Sydelle! So good to see you again!
Syd, get out of here!

SNAP!
Syd!
Ughhh
I'm disappointed, Wayland.
I always warned you not to let your guard down.

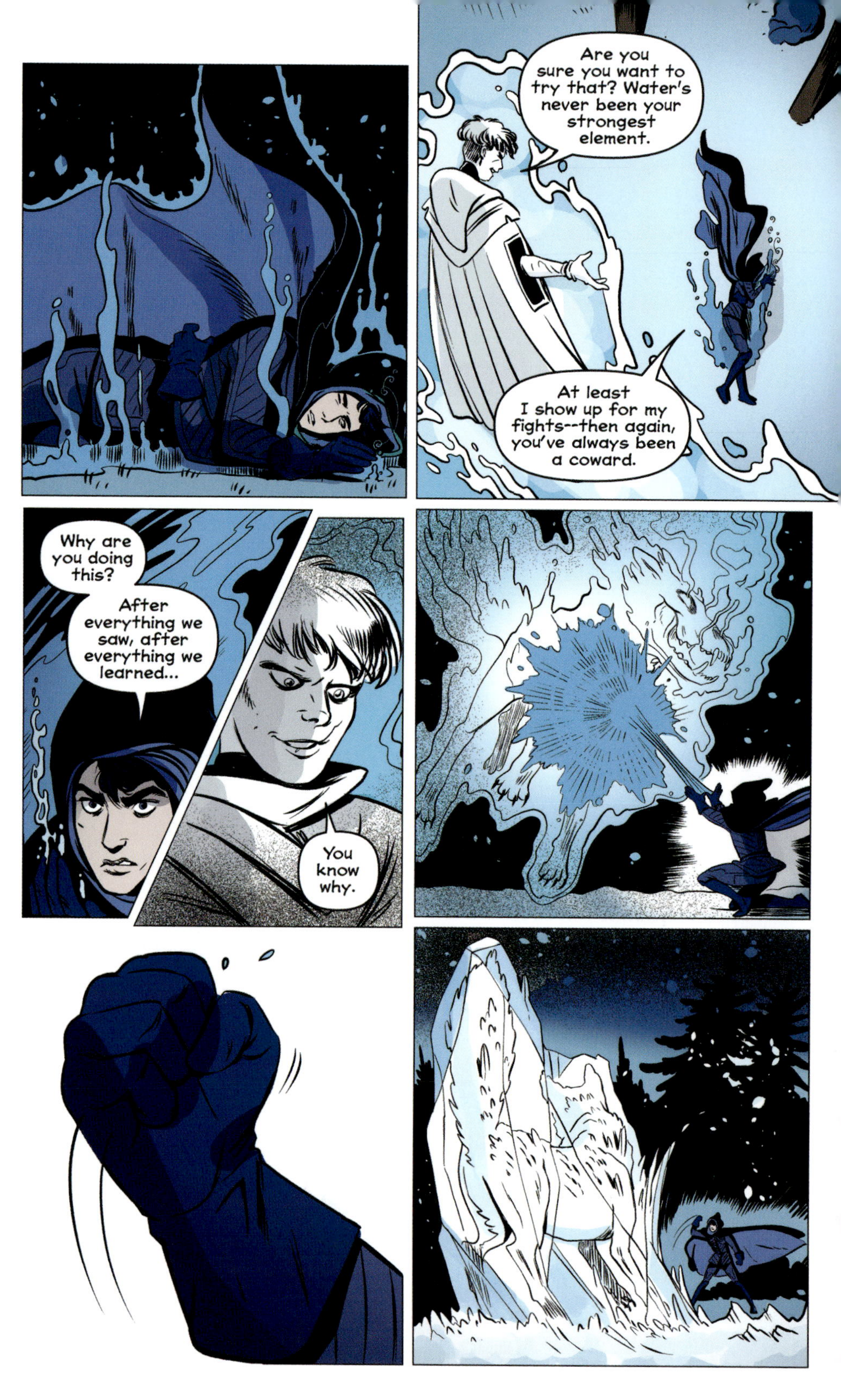

Are you sure you want to try that? Water's never been your strongest element.
At least I show up for my fights--then again, you've always been a coward.
Why are you doing this?
After everything we saw, after everything we learned...
You know why.

Here!

RUUURUUUUMMMMBBBBLLLEE

RUUUUMMMBBBBLLE!

Owwww...
Are you all right?
I'm fine.
What about Dorwan? Is he dead?
We should be so lucky.
He projected himself magically. It'll be a while before he can use a spell like that again, though. I hit him with enough to hurt him, at the very least.
You're lucky. It doesn't look that bad.
Yeah...

Oh-- I can wash that--
Nah, I got it.
How badly are you hurt?
I've been better.
Come on. I'll help you get back to the house.

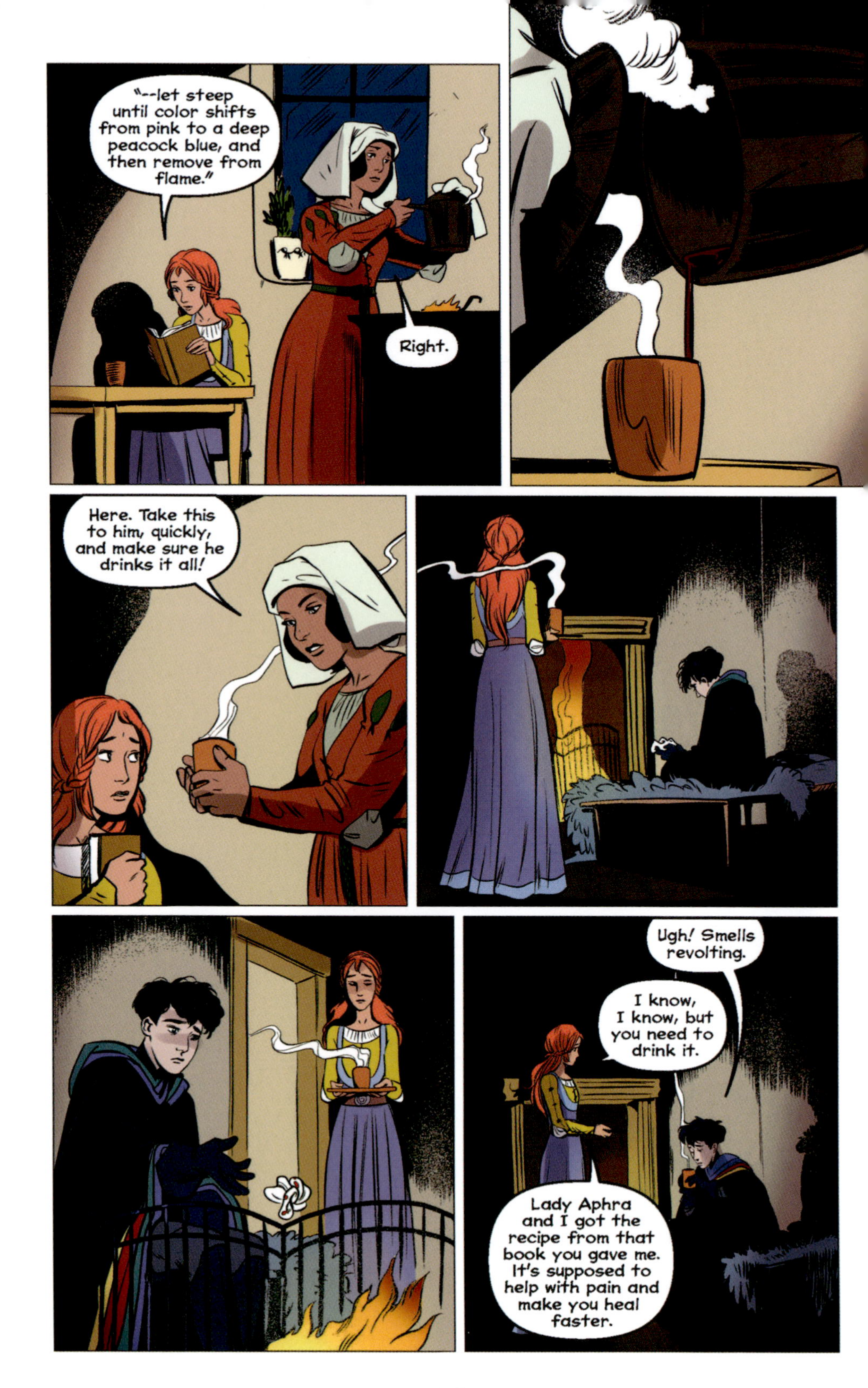
"--let steep until color shifts from pink to a deep peacock blue, and then remove from flame."
Right.
Here. Take this to him, quickly, and make sure he drinks it all!
Ugh! Smells revolting.
I know, I know, but you need to drink it.
Lady Aphra and I got the recipe from that book you gave me. It's supposed to help with pain and make you heal faster.

Thanks, Syd.
Just need t' take a nap...
ZZZZZZ
He'll be out for a while. Let's get him tucked in.
I'll get his boots and socks, you get his cloaks and gloves.
Gasp!

Lady Aphra, what--
He didn't tell you, then?
What's wrong with him?
His great-grandfather was cursed by a dark wizard he was trying to bring to justice. It only affects the sons in Wayland's family line.
It took his father from us ten years ago. You'll have to ask him for the whole story, though.
He's never told it to me.
Is there any cure?
No, Miss Mirabil. No cure.
Wayland's father and grandfather spent their entire lives looking for one.

Who are you?

Ah, you're awake.
My name is Pascal. I'm Wayland's magic instructor.
Come along, Miss Mirabil. Lady Aphra's prepared breakfast for us.
He'll be all right. I've given him another potion, one that'll speed his recovery. He'll sleep for another few hours at least.

Here, let me.
Thank you.
Come sit and eat something, Sydelle. I won't have anyone wasting away in my house.
Hear, hear!
That goes for you, too, you old crow. When was the last time you had a decent meal?
It's been a few weeks.

Is North really going to be all right?
Physically? Yes. Spiritually? I'm not sure.
He's struggling with himself.
I'm concerned he's been holding himself back, and that's why he hasn't been able to defeat Dorwan.
Aphra tells me that you know about the curse affecting Wayland's family.
Yes.
I'm afraid that, since his father's death, Wayland's managed to convince himself that magic is nothing more than pain and destruction. It's hurt his ability to use his magic effectively.
I need to persuade him to come back to the Wizard Guard.
We're his best chance at finding a cure for his curse.
But you're his instructor! Don't you tell him about Astraea's teachings? His magic is more than a gift--it's a true blessing!
Not to him.
Whatever you may believe, Miss Mirabil, magic is a responsibility, a burden, and a duty. You don't choose to have it.
Indeed. Very few of us would, given the choice.

Some wizards seem to enjoy having power.
You're referring to Dorwan?
Yes. I've often wondered if magic isn't a weight for him, as well, not to mention being judged for his father's crime.
Crime?
His father led a short-lived coup against the king.
That was ***his*** father?
Unfortunately, yes.
I remember hearing about the execution...
Magic is a tool. It exists everywhere, all the time, and it ***demands*** to be used...
...one way or the other. And we wizards must learn to master it. We must open ourselves to it, yet never allow it out of our control. Otherwise it'll control ***us***.
I think Dorwan has forgotten that, if he ever knew it.
My greatest fear is that North will forget it, as well.

Lady Aphra! A letter came! For Miss Mirabil.
Who is it from?
From my parents. From home!

We love you and we miss you. Astraea keep you safe! Write again when you can!

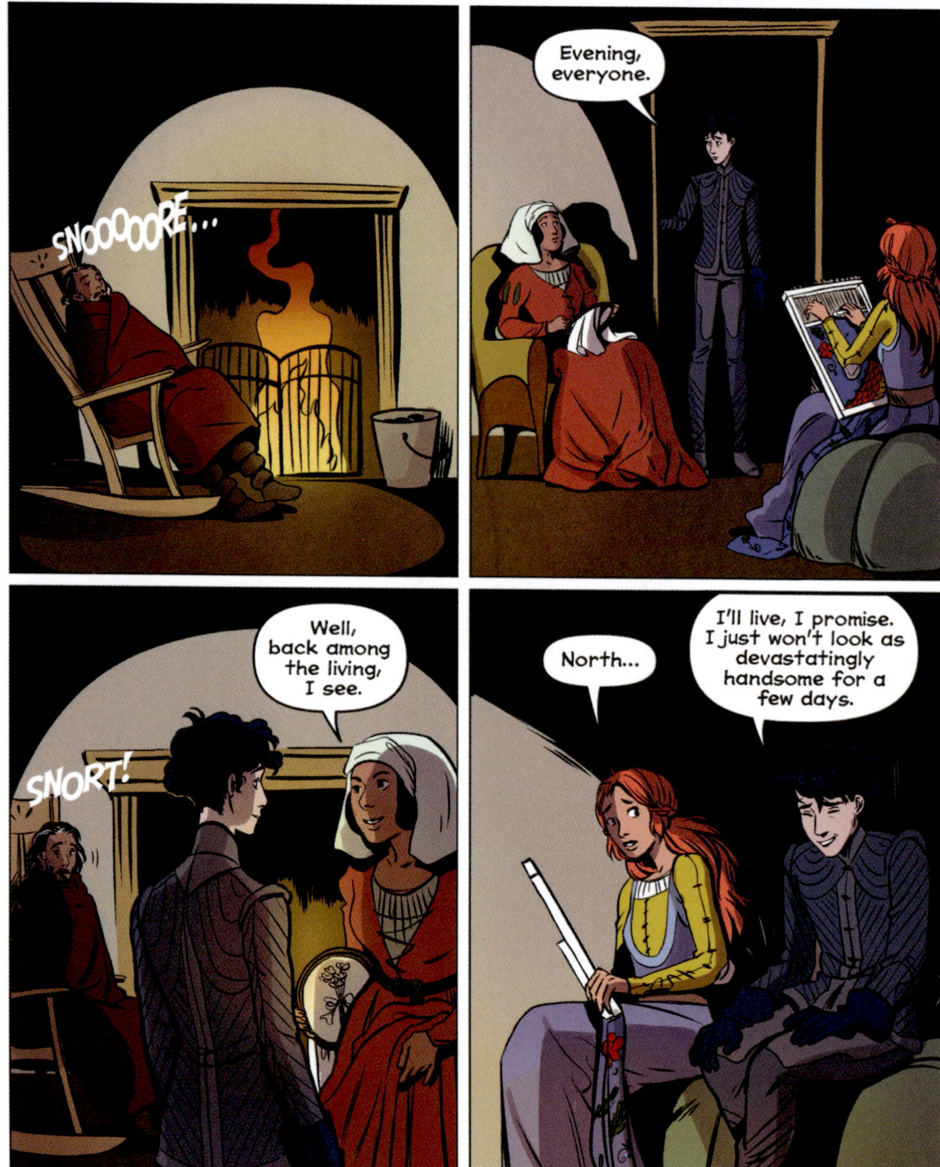
SNOOOOORE...
Evening, everyone.
SNORT!
Well, back among the living, I see.
North...
I'll live, I promise. I just won't look as devastatingly handsome for a few days.

Dorwan got away.
I know, Wayland. Do you want to tell us what happened?
That creature Dorwan called up was a shade. I should have just banished it the moment it appeared, but I was hoping I could trace him through it.
I--I just couldn't get the magic to obey me.

Sigh!
I guess I was outclassed.
Pfft! Ridiculous! You're *my* student. You're worth ten Dorwans. Magic tracing is hard, that's all.
C'mon! I'll give you a quick refresher!
I need to make the rounds in the children's dormitories and ensure everything's ready for their lunch. I'll be back in an hour or so.
Do you want any help?

Thank you, my girl, but that's quite all right.

You know he's strongest with the water magic, so look for knots of blue and white.
I-- I can't.
Don't be afraid. You're holding yourself back.
It's getting worse, isn't it? Every time I use magic, the curse sets in deeper. It eats a little more of me. I've never felt so weak.

I don't remember it affecting my father this way. His magic always seemed so strong... up until the end....
You're just as strong as he was. He was just better at hiding how much he struggled.
Dorwan won't be content until all Palmarta's wizards have been destroyed.
And a war with Auster is the best way to do that.
He'll do anything to keep me from delivering my report.
"I think once...he really did want to prove himself to achieve a high rank in the Wizard Guard.
"Now, I think he'll do anything for power, including turning against his own country and destroying anyone who stands in his way."
But after this fight... I don't think I can stand against him.
What about using...
No!
Wayland!

Come on, Syd, we're leaving.
Wh-what? Now? Just like that?

Just like that. Get your things.

Wayland, think about this, please. Come back to the Wizard Guard. Let us see if we can find another way to help you!
My report's more important, and we're running out of time.

Say good-bye to Lady Aphra for me.
Unh!
I thought I could get us farther than this.

What were you and Pascal arguing about?
Nothing.
We need to get moving. With Dorwan skulking around, I can't risk him tracing my spell.
Don't tell me that was nothing!
Why won't you let the other wizards help you?!
Because it's my responsibility!
What do you mean, "your responsibility"?

I've been by your side this entire journey. You owe me an explanation. You didn't even tell me about your family's curse!
I... Y-you're right. You're right.
"When Dorwan and I first met during our training, we were disillusioned with the Wizard Guard. I was upset they hadn't been able to cure my father, and a lot of our instructors and the other students treated Dorwan poorly because of what his father had done."

I thought Dorwan and I were a lot alike. That we were kindred spirits, I guess.
I let him convince me that we could find a cure for my family curse by delving into forbidden magic.
"Then I realized he was just using me to help him create magically infused poisons. He tried to use one against me before I could report him."
Is that why you're so certain he's the one who poisoned the king?
Yes.
"When the king died, no one recognized the poison. They assumed it was foreign. But I recognized it."
Because it was the one he'd used on you?
Yes. And I barely managed to counter it.

Is that what's in your report? You have proof that Dorwan's behind the poison?
Yes. The Wizard Guard may have a lot of good points, but they've also got plenty of bad ones. They're stubborn. Proud. Entrenched in their belief in their own infallibility.
The king's murder was a hard blow to their egos. And to expect them to believe, on my word alone, that an unranked dark stripling of a wizard got the better of them?
They'd never listen to me. I knew unless I had proof--good, solid proof--there's no way they'd believe me. I...don't exactly have a sterling reputation in the capital.
You should have told me! What if Dorwan managed to kill you? He could sway the vote by poisoning more people, like Queen Eglantine!
Did you tell Owain? Or Pascal? Lady Aphra? Anyone?!
I can't! I'm afraid Dorwan will go after anyone I share the report with!
What were you thinking? This information is important! It's bigger than both of us!
I underestimated Dorwan once and he poisoned our king. I know what he's really capable of. How much hatred he has.
I won't underestimate him again.
North, wait!
North!

LATER...
WHAM!
There!
You look terrible.
I'm fine!
WHUMPH!
No way Dorwan's going to be able to sneak up on us tonight. Nothing's going to be able to get past those wards without me knowing.
Just going to sleep for a little bit. Wake me up in a few hours, all right?
Sure.

"Proper concentration for casting spells...herbs for potions and elixirs... magically inclined humans?"
"Magically inclined humans often have wizards far back in their family lines. They often make excellent assistants for their abilities to mix potions and repair magical talismans."
MIRABIL/ CLIFFTON
VIII
Jinxes
Did he come to Cliffton *looking* for my family?!

Those soldiers only came because of him!
He said it would hide me from Dorwan.

It's the report that matters, not him, and not me.

Ugh!
Astraea be with me.

Thank you for everything, old friend....

Syd!

Syd-elle!

Sydelle, why--
I know what you haven't been telling me.

You came to Cliffton on purpose because you wanted to find someone who could fix your talismans!
MIRABIL/ CLIFFTON
VIII
Jinxes

You led those soldiers right to us!
I'm sorry, Syd. My cloaks were so damaged...and Dorwan was right behind me... I didn't think I had a choice.
But I meant what I said when I told you the choice was yours. If you'd wanted to go back to your village, I wouldn't have stopped you.
How can we work together if you insist on keeping secrets from me?!

Fair?
Fair!
Your book is fine, you know. It's in my bag.
I figured.
Where'd you find this horse, anyway?
I rented it from a merchant I ran into.
Ha!
What?
I'm just surprised you didn't get lost.
Noooooooorth...
The merchant told me the horse knows his way back to the capital.

Hey, where's your loom?
I--I had to use the wood for something else.
I'm sorry. Truly.
It's all right. I don't think I'll have much time to weave in Provincia anyway.

My friends!
Owain!
What are you doing here?!
I tried to tell the Wizard Guard they have to delay the vote, but they wouldn't listen to me!
Finally I gave up and decided to come here to wait for you two!
I'm sorry, Owain. I knew they'd be difficult.
Well, never mind that. I decided to come here and do what I could to speed your journey. I rented us a wagon and a good strong horse.

The innkeeper said he'll keep the horse until his owner comes back through.
Good. That poor horse needs a rest, anyway.
There's only one day until the vote. We need to meet with the Sorceress Imperial as soon as possible.
Giddyap!

PROVINCIA

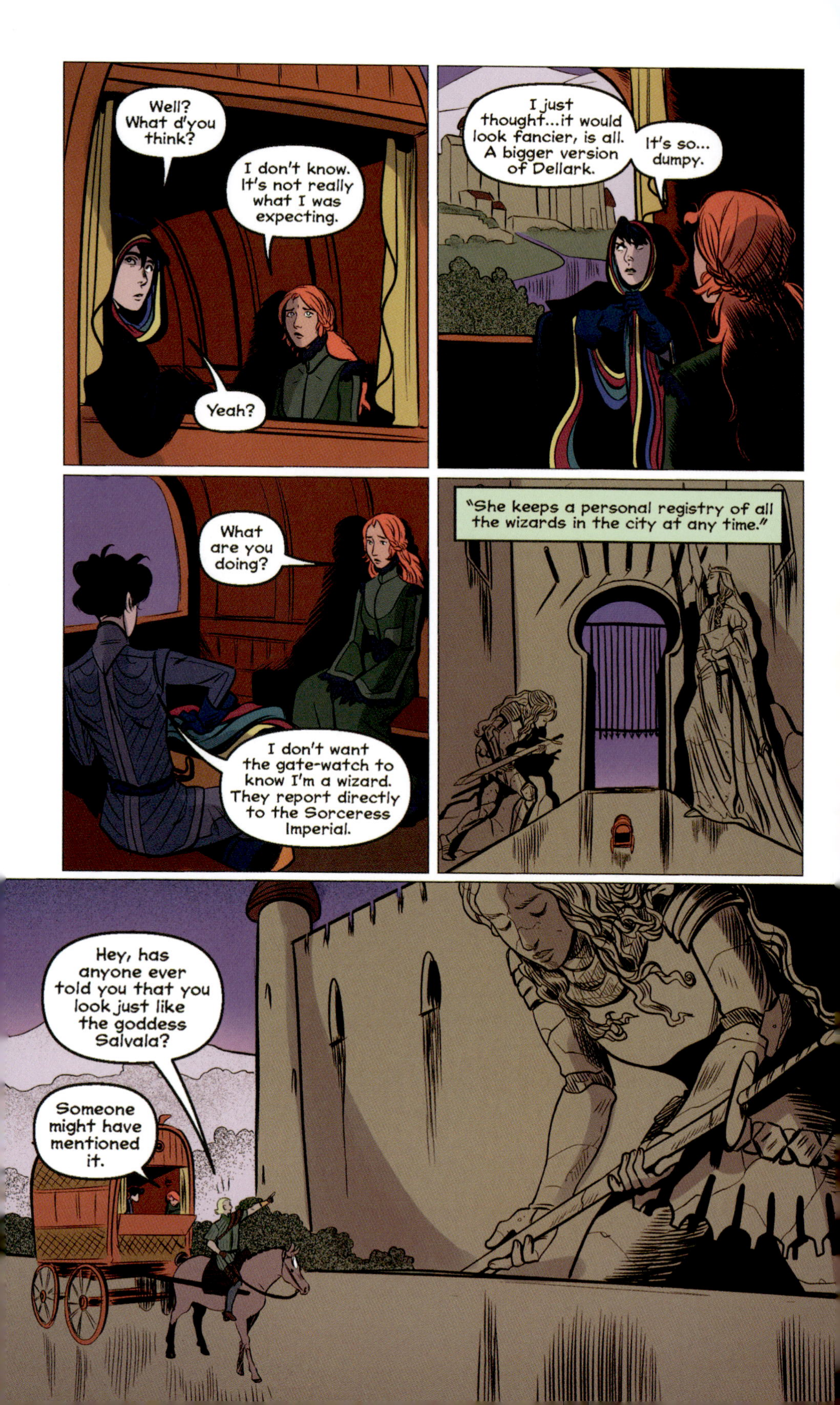
Well? What d'you think?
I don't know. It's not really what I was expecting.
Yeah?
I just thought...it would look fancier, is all. A bigger version of Dellark.
It's so... dumpy.
What are you doing?
I don't want the gate-watch to know I'm a wizard. They report directly to the Sorceress Imperial.
"She keeps a personal registry of all the wizards in the city at any time."
Hey, has anyone ever told you that you look just like the goddess Salvala?
Someone might have mentioned it.

Man or wizard?
Man.
And you?
Man, of course.
And this is my little sister, Sarah.
Head in, then.
Curfew starts in one hour!
Sure thing!

This is as close as we're going to be able to get.
Owain, you'll have to wait here. It's hard enough to twist with one other person. There's no way I can manage it with two.

The Sorceress Imperial!

Wayland!
What do you think you're doing?!
Hey, Ollie.
Close your mouth, Ollie. She's a friend of mine.
Sydelle, this is Oliver. He's a former classmate of mine.
This is a surprise.
Hello, Mother.
!

I--I didn't know...
That I was related to someone important?
No! It's just...
She's so...
And I'm so...
That's not what I meant.
Mother, this is Sydelle Mirabil, formerly of Cliffton.
Assistant-slash-navigator.

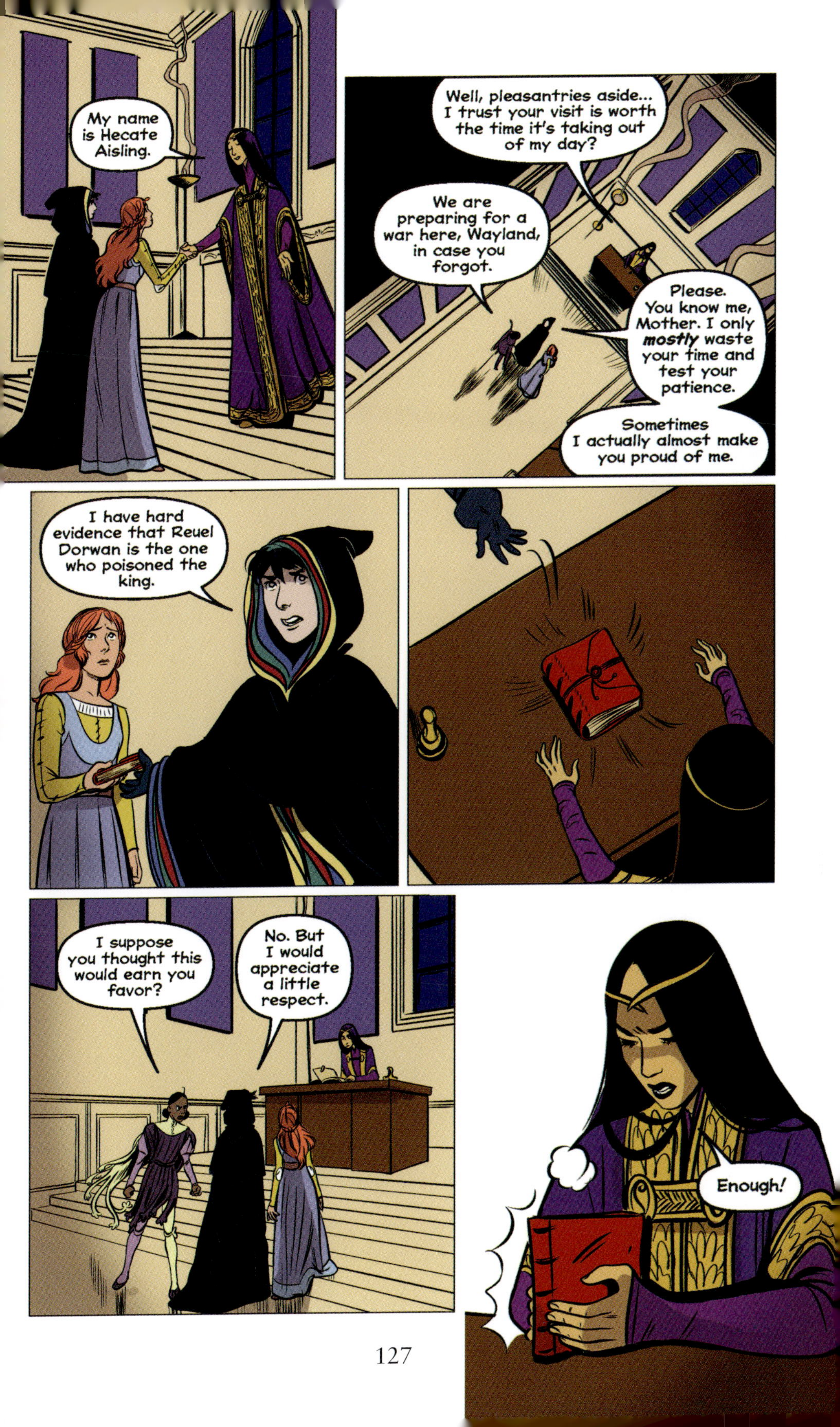
My name is Hecate Aisling.
Well, pleasantries aside... I trust your visit is worth the time it's taking out of my day?
We are preparing for a war here, Wayland, in case you forgot.
Please. You know me, Mother. I only **mostly** waste your time and test your patience.
Sometimes I actually almost make you proud of me.
I have hard evidence that Reuel Dorwan is the one who poisoned the king.
I suppose you thought this would earn you favor?
No. But I would appreciate a little respect.
Enough!

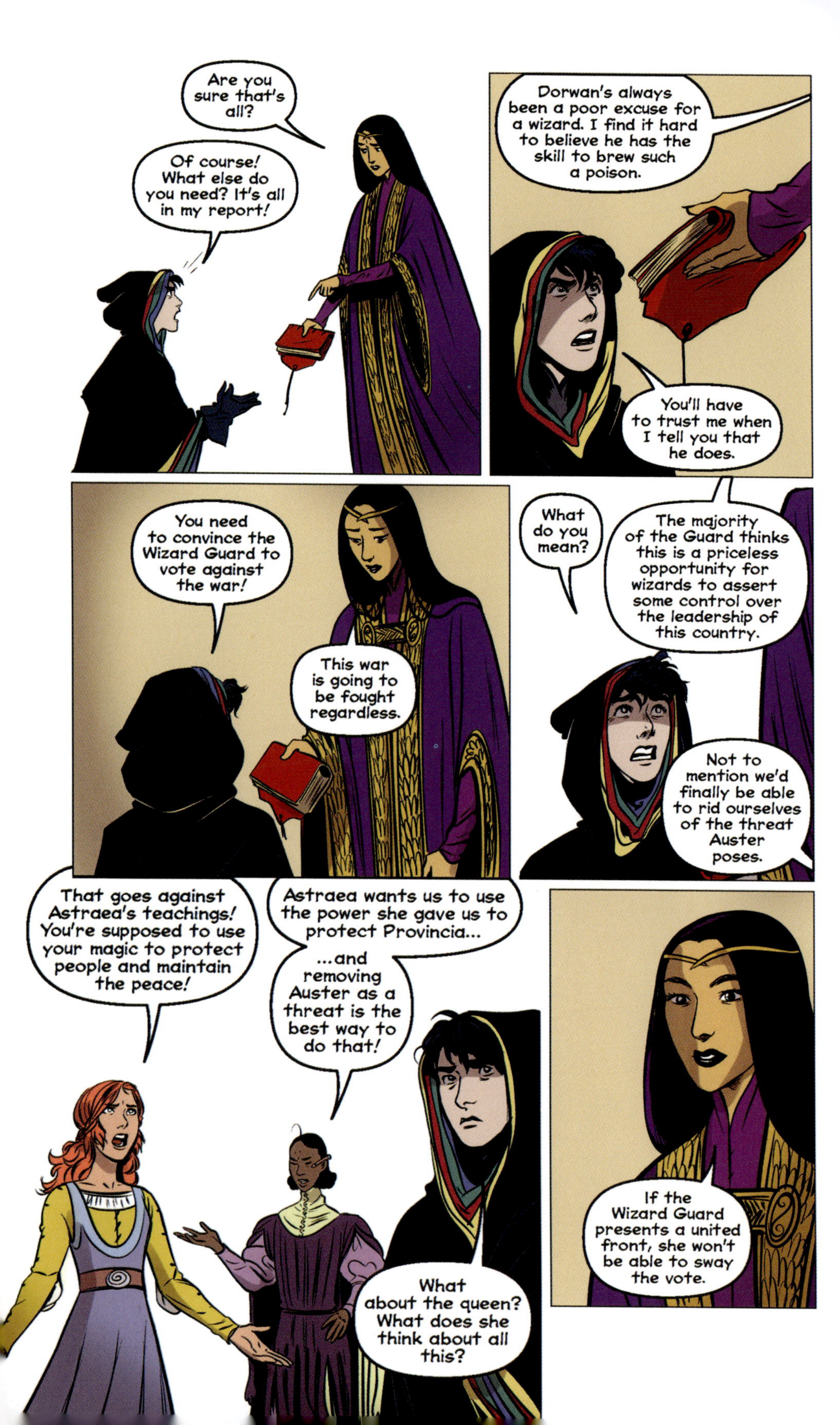
Are you sure that's all?
Of course! What else do you need? It's all in my report!
Dorwan's always been a poor excuse for a wizard. I find it hard to believe he has the skill to brew such a poison.
You'll have to trust me when I tell you that he does.
You need to convince the Wizard Guard to vote against the war!
This war is going to be fought regardless.
What do you mean?
The majority of the Guard thinks this is a priceless opportunity for wizards to assert some control over the leadership of this country.
Not to mention we'd finally be able to rid ourselves of the threat Auster poses.
That goes against Astraea's teachings! You're supposed to use your magic to protect people and maintain the peace!
Astraea wants us to use the power she gave us to protect Provincia...
...and removing Auster as a threat is the best way to do that!
What about the queen? What does she think about all this?
If the Wizard Guard presents a united front, she won't be able to sway the vote.

So you'll start a war over nothing?! Thousands of people could die!
Control your pet, Wayland.
No one speaks to the Sorceress Imperial in that tone.
It's fine, Oliver. I'm accustomed to tantrums.
We didn't come all this way just so you could force Palmarta into a war!
And what if the Austerans manage to win against us?
We have magic, but they have a stronger military! What then?
You know they despise wizards! They'll do whatever it takes to crush every last one of us!
Well, isn't that the reason you brought her? To use against Auster?
Or did you think that pathetic little charm of yours could hide her from every wizard in the capital?
Were you planning to keep her for yourself?
North, what...?
Haven't you told her she's a jinx?
I-I'm just magically inclined!

You're much more than that.
A jinx is a human who can generate magic without the ability to control it.
"Storms."
"Earthquakes."
"Fires."
"Droughts."
Jinxes unintentionally create them all.
Syd, wait!

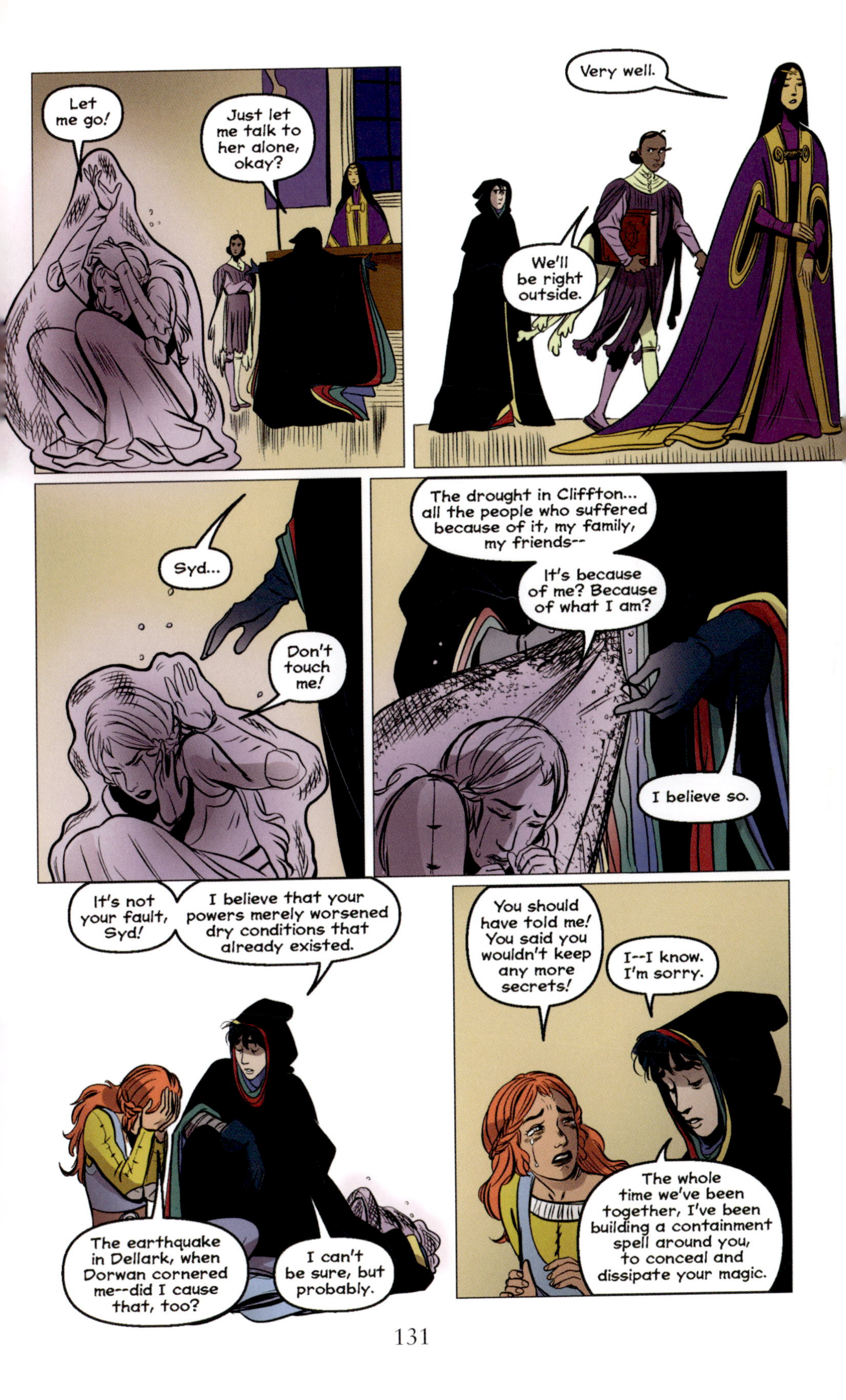

Let me go!
Just let me talk to her alone, okay?
Very well.
We'll be right outside.
Syd...
Don't touch me!
The drought in Cliffton... all the people who suffered because of it, my family, my friends--
It's because of me? Because of what I am?
I believe so.
It's not your fault, Syd!
I believe that your powers merely worsened dry conditions that already existed.
The earthquake in Dellark, when Dorwan cornered me--did I cause that, too?
I can't be sure, but probably.
You should have told me! You said you wouldn't keep any more secrets!
I--I know. I'm sorry.
The whole time we've been together, I've been building a containment spell around you, to conceal and dissipate your magic.

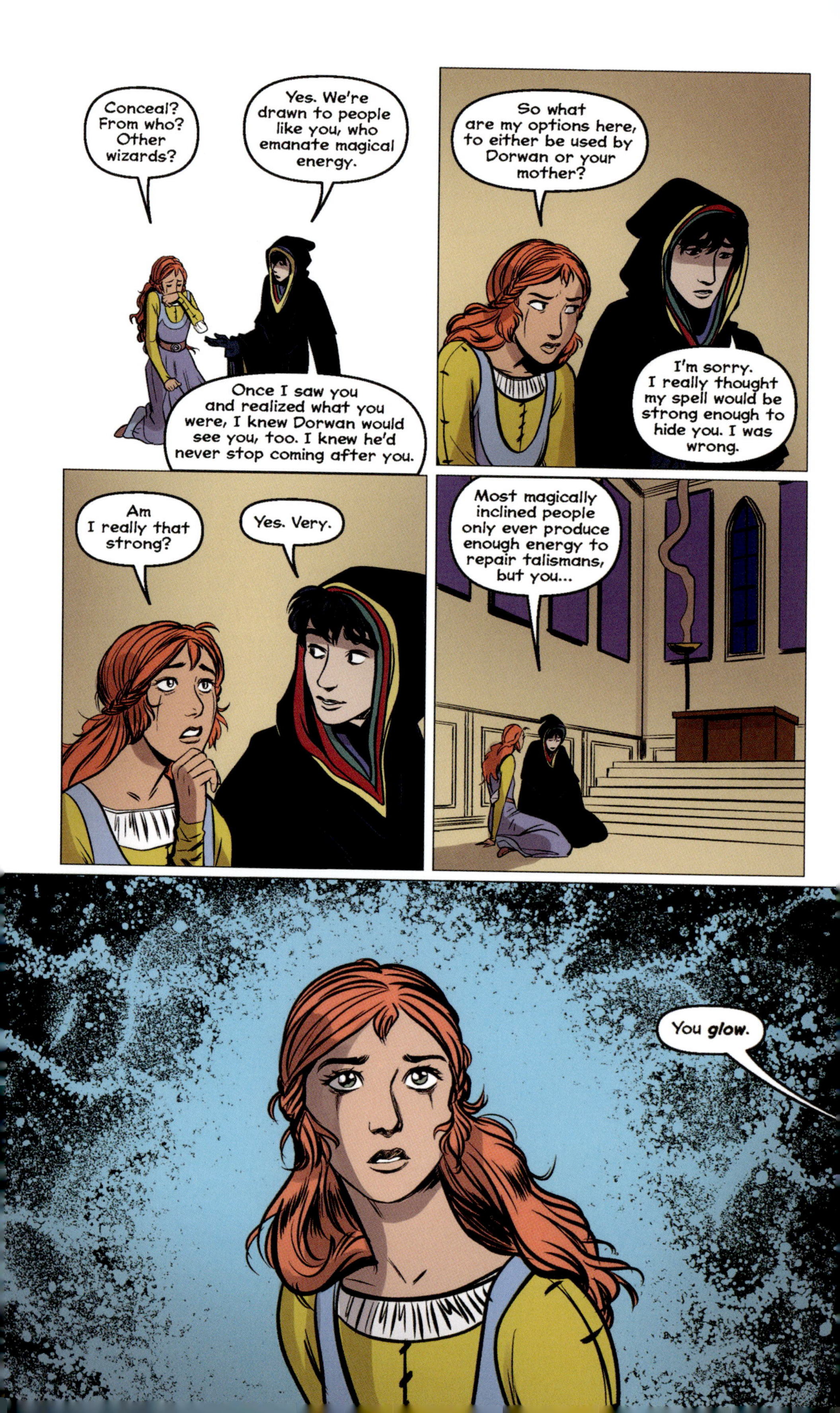
Conceal? From who? Other wizards?
Yes. We're drawn to people like you, who emanate magical energy.
Once I saw you and realized what you were, I knew Dorwan would see you, too. I knew he'd never stop coming after you.
So what are my options here, to either be used by Dorwan or your mother?
I'm sorry. I really thought my spell would be strong enough to hide you. I was wrong.
Am I really that strong?
Yes. Very.
Most magically inclined people only ever produce enough energy to repair talismans, but you...
You *glow*.

So what happens to me now?
We'll figure something out! I'm certainly not going to let my mother use you--
It's like I always told you, Wayland...
Never let your guard down.

Goddess Salvala! This humble and obedient king welcomes you to your kingdom.
Welcome to Auster!

Wh-what?
A moment, my lord.
The living avatar of the goddess has only recently awoken to her true self. She's still confused.
I'm presenting you as the living embodiment of the goddess Salvala.
You know, Astraea's red-haired, magic-spurning, sword-loving sister.
I know who Salvala is!
If I were you, I'd go along with it.
Otherwise the king will execute us both.
Great Lady, our legends speak of a beautiful girl with the ability to harness the power of storms and calamity!
Bah! Can't you see, she has no idea what you're talking about!
She's no goddess! I told you not to trust the wizard!
Silence! I'll not have you speak to her so!
Auster is her home now, and she will be celebrated and loved here.
Indeed, with her by your side, no one in Palmarta--wizard or otherwise--will be able to stand against you.
I can't--
She doesn't understand the holy tongue!

Is this true?!
Have you brought me a false goddess?
I have brought you the goddess of destruction herself. She's everything you need to crush Palmarta and their wizards.
Liar! Demon!
Don't think your magic will save you, wizard. Their weapons are charmed.
Wait!

I'll prove myself to you.
Fine. I have a challenge worthy of a goddess.
But if you fail, I'll cut off both your heads and feed your bodies to my dogs.

Bring it down, Great Lady. Use your power to reduce this mountain to rubble, and I will allow no one to question your divinity.
You heard the king, Sydelle.
Shut up, Dorwan.
Every time my power's manifested I was frightened or angry...but it wasn't a conscious decision.
What if I can't do it on command?
No. Don't think that.
Pascal said magic is a tool. That wizards open themselves to it.

Sydelle!
Don't touch me.

You shouldn't have let your guard down.
WHOOOOOOOOSH!!
Aaahh!
KAH-TOOM!
Look!

RUUURUUUUMMMBBBLLLEE!
Salvala...
My Lord! We must leave!
Get him out of here!

Huf!
Oof!
SYDELLE!

Syd!
Jump!

FLAP!
North!!!
How did you find me?
I could practically *see* all the magic you created! It was like you were a star burning on the mountaintop.

Are you all right? Where's Dorwan? Did he hurt you?
I don't think you need to worry about him.
I blew him over the side of the cliff and brought most of the snow on this mountain down on top of him.
Guess he shouldn't have let his guard down.
Ahaaha hahahaha!
Syd, you're amazing!

Let's get out of here!
Wait!

The vote's today, isn't it?
Yeah. It's going to be soon. Within the hour, for certain.

Is your mother going to be there?

PROVINCIA
And now the Sorceress Imperial will present intelligence she's gathered in support of the assertion that Auster is behind the king's assassination.

Wayland!

Madame Sorceress! We stand ready to report on the situation in Auster!
This is too much--
It's all right, Oliver.
Madam Secretary, may we call a recess?
That won't be necessary.
We have a peace treaty signed by the king of Auster himself.
Declaration

This is the royal house's official seal!
How--
Using every diplomatic tool at my disposal, I was able to secure an audience with the king.
"Miss Mirabil acted as a representative of the people of Cliffton, one of the first towns that would be affected by a war with Auster."
"She delivered a powerful appeal to the king's sense of basic human dignity."
"The Austerans are eager to avoid a war."

CLAP CLAP!

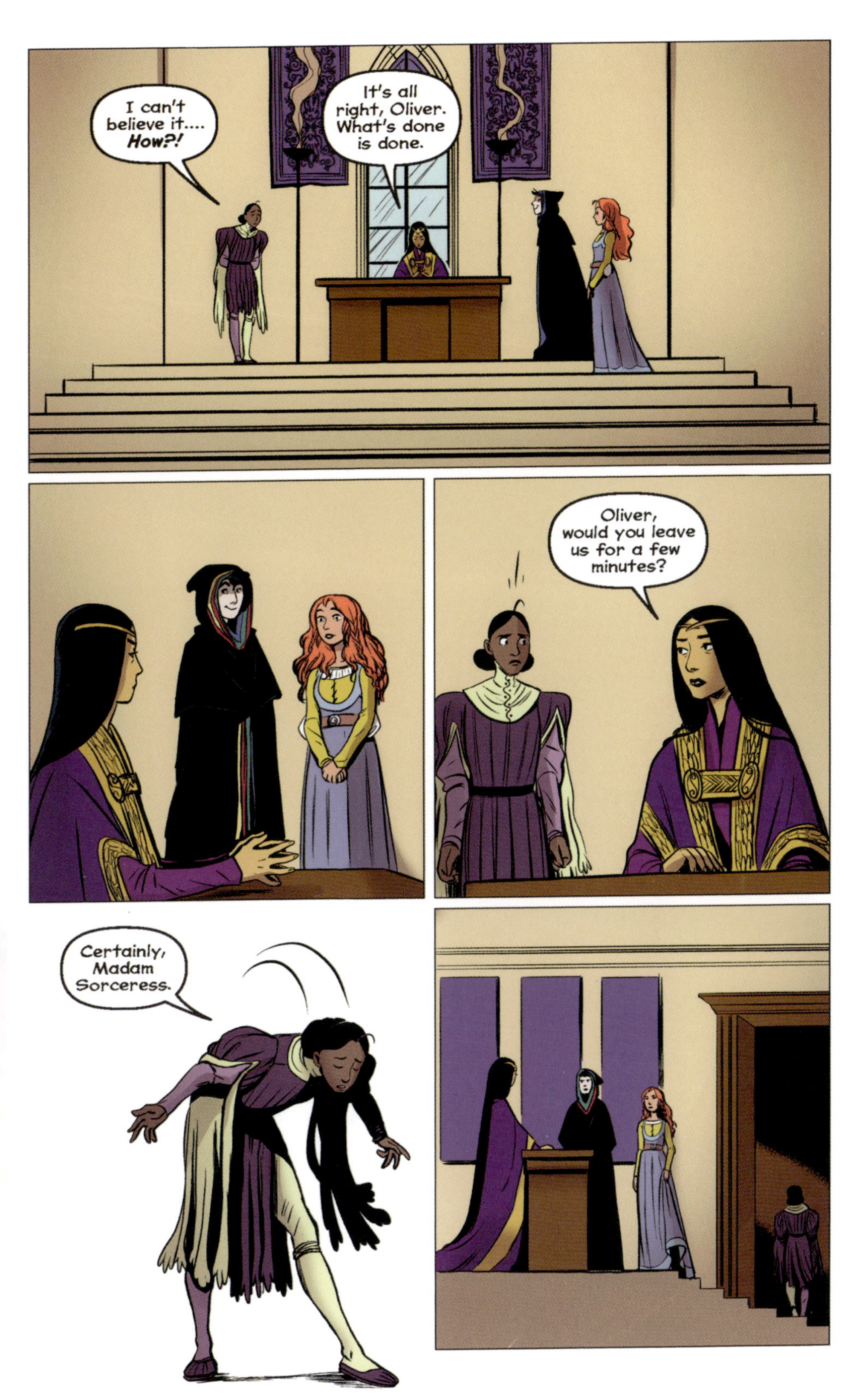
I can't believe it.... **How?!**
It's all right, Oliver. What's done is done.
Oliver, would you leave us for a few minutes?
Certainly, Madam Sorceress.

I'm not going to ask exactly how you were able to secure that treaty.
I am going to ask you what you propose to do about Miss Mirabil.
You know the danger she'll face from other wizards who may be tempted to try to use her power themselves.
Not to mention, I don't think the Guard is going to be willing to let you just wander around once they realize what you are.
I can offer you protection here, at Wizard Command. I might even be legally required to do so.
I don't want protection.
I want a chance to learn how to use my power properly.
That's fair.

I've spent a lot of time lately in the Guard's archives, searching for a possible cure for Wayland.
I discovered evidence of an ancient library far to the north, which may contain volumes that have been missing from Provincia's libraries for centuries.
Of course, the north is very isolated. I doubt anyone would notice if there was the occasional storm or earthquake.

What's keeping Owain?
He'll be along.

He's just picking something up for me.
Then I suppose this is as good a time as any.
For what?
I have something for you.
SNAP!

Syd! It's beautiful!
Every color is used equally.
You're lucky I finished it before I had to burn my loom.

I was this close to selling it to the highest-bidding wizard, but I decided to give it to you instead.
I love it! Thank you!
What ho, fellow adventurers! What a perfect day to begin such a journey!
Ah! Perfect timing.

Did you get it?
I'll ride ahead a bit.
So what's that about?
I got you something, too.

My loom! But how--
I drew up the plans from memory and found a local craftswoman who could do the work.
Thank you.

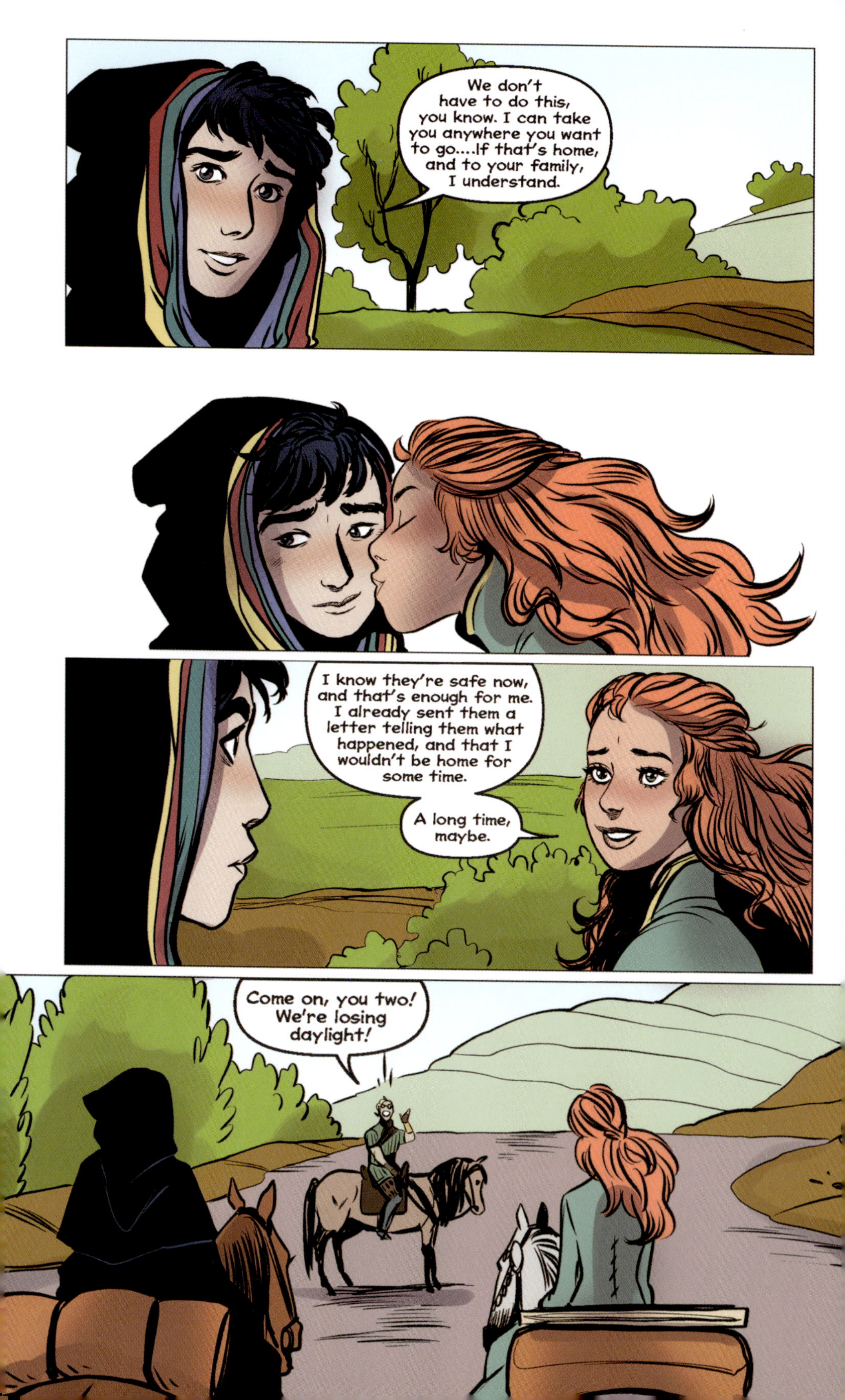

We don't have to do this, you know. I can take you anywhere you want to go....If that's home, and to your family, I understand.
I know they're safe now, and that's enough for me. I already sent them a letter telling them what happened, and that I wouldn't be home for some time.
A long time, maybe.
Come on, you two! We're losing daylight!

You ready?

ACKNOWLEDGMENTS:

First and foremost, thank you so much to Leigh Dragoon and Kit Seaton for bringing this story to life in such loving, fun detail. It was such a pleasure to work with you both, and I can't begin to express how grateful I am to you for taking such great care of the characters and story. Thank you to Hannah Allaman, editor extraordinaire, for leading us all on this adventure together, as well as to Marci Senders, Whiteley Foster, and David William for all of your hard work in putting this project together. As always, I'm incredibly grateful to the whole team at Disney Hyperion for truly making the magic happen, to Merrilee Heifetz for never leading me astray, and to my family and friends for all of your love and support over this ten-year journey. And, finally, thank you to Carlin for inspiring me to actually sit down and draft the original book when I thought I might never write another one. —A.B.

I'd like to acknowledge all the colleagues and faculty where I have studied and taught. Their tireless dedication to education in the arts continues to inspire me, and without their support and advice, I would still be standing on the sidelines. I would also like to acknowledge my sister for completing her Peace Corps service, and my beautiful mother, who survived cancer this year.

—K.S.

ALEXANDRA BRACKEN is the No. 1 *New York Times* bestselling author of the Darkest Minds series. Born and raised in Arizona, she moved east to study history and English at the College of William & Mary in Virginia. After working in publishing for several years, Alex now writes full-time and can be found hard at work on her next novel in a charming little home that's perpetually overflowing with books. Visit her online at www.alexandrabracken.com and on Twitter @alexbracken.

LEIGH DRAGOON was raised in a log cabin in the Adirondacks, where she developed an early love of reading and writing. She became a fan of *Little Women* at age nine, after Beth's demise made her bawl herself to sleep. This led to a lifelong appreciation of the book. After years of annual rereads, she also became fascinated with learning about Louisa May and her family. Leigh has several print publications of her own, both graphic novels and prose, through HarperCollins and Penguin. She adapted both Richelle Mead's Vampire Academy and Marie Lu's Legend series into graphic-novel scripts. She has also written three Adventure Time prose novels: *Queen of Rogues*, *The Lonesome Outlaw*, and *The Virtue of Ardor*, and has created original comics stories and scripts for Mattel's *Ever After High* and Disney's *Tangled*.

KIT SEATON grew up on a steady diet of comic strips, '80s cartoons, and volumes of illustrated fairy-tale books. She bused tables, sold computers, slung coffee, directed plays, and designed costumes before finally finding her home illustrating comic books. Kit earned her master's in illustration from the Hartford Art School and has taught comics and illustration at Rocky Mountain College of Art + Design, Savannah College of Art and Design, and California State University, Fullerton. She makes her home with an old snuggle-grump house cat named Gus and a puppy named Panya in the Inland Northwest.